THE
SMALLEST
TURTLE

Scholastic Publications Ltd,
10 Earlham Street, London WC2H 9RX, UK

Scholastic Inc.,
730 Broadway, New York, NY 10003, USA

Scholastic Canada Ltd,
123 Newkirk Road, Richmond Hill,
Ontario L4C 3G5, Canada

Ashton Scholastic Pty. Ltd,
P O Box 579, Gosford, New South Wales,
Australia

Ashton Scholastic Ltd,
Private Bag 1, Penrose, Auckland,
New Zealand

First published by Mallinson Rendell Publishers Ltd, 1982
First published in paperback by Scholastic Publications Ltd, 1991

Text copyright © Lynley Dodd, 1982

ISBN 0 590 76525 6

THE
SMALLEST
TURTLE

Lynley Dodd

Hippo Books
Scholastic Publications Limited
London

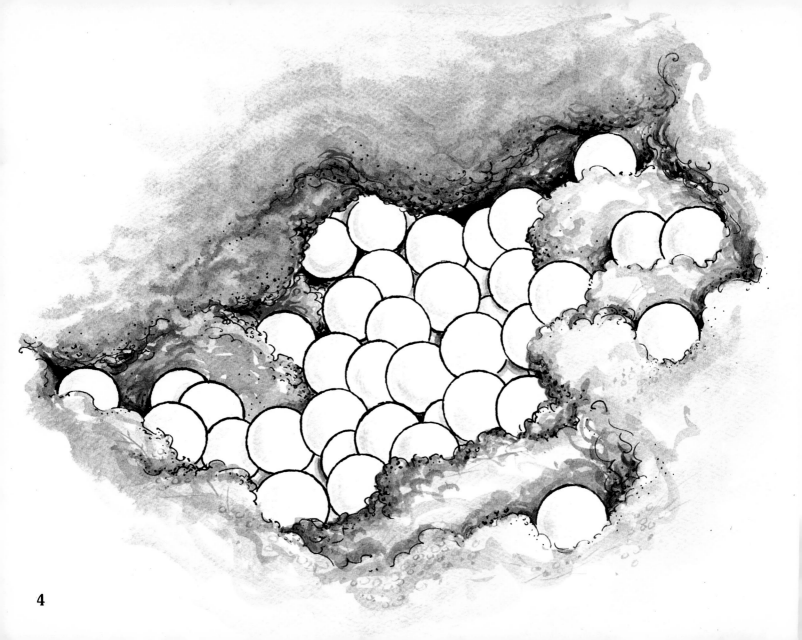

Deep in a safe dark hole
under the sand
lay a nest of turtle eggs.

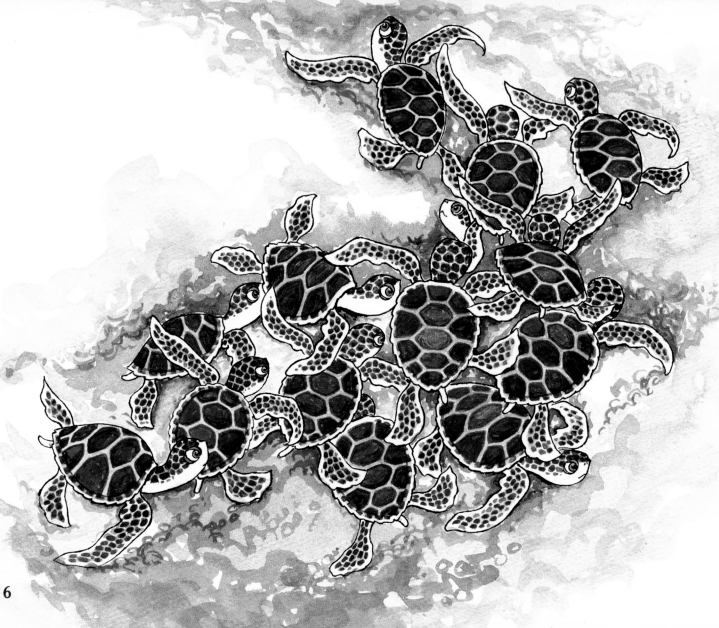

One day,
they began to hatch.
Soon there were
dozens of baby turtles
all wriggling together
up through the sand
and away.

Except the smallest turtle.
He was late.
All by himself
he scrambled and scrabbled
up, up, up . . .

and out into the shimmery sun.
He blinked at the brightness
and inside his head he heard strange words,
'To the sea — to the sea.'

So away he went,
skitterscatter,
over a shiny grey rock
and past a big black beetle,

around a tree with twisty roots,

down a gravelly hole
and up the other side,
where a sleepy lizard
was dozing in the sun,

18

through some prickly grass
where a spider was weaving a web
and all the time, his head said,
'To the sea — to the sea'.

The sun was burning down
on the smallest turtle.
It made him too hot
and it muddled the words in his head.
He began to go round and round
in circles.

He crept into the shade
of a big green leaf
to cool down
and as he cooled,
the words in his head
slowly came back again,
'To the sea — to the sea'.

So on and on went the smallest turtle
until at last he stopped to rest.
He was getting very tired.
Suddenly he heard something.
It was the sound of waves
crashing and hissing on the sand.
The words in his head became stronger than ever,
'To the SEA — to the SEA.'

But there was danger.
Gulls were wheeling and whirling
up in the sky,
looking with beady greedy eyes
for a baby turtle lunch.

The smallest turtle didn't wait.
Down the scorching sand he scrabbled and skittered,
faster, faster,
away from the gulls,
past the crabs,
over the seaweed,
over the shells,
over the stones and . . .

at last he felt cool cool water
on his hot tired sandy body.
And as he swam down,
down,
down,
he knew.
'It's the SEA', he sang,
'It's the SEA!'

Acknowledgement
This book was written with the assistance of the Choysa Bursary,
funded jointly by Quality Packers Ltd. and the New Zealand Literary Fund.
The author gratefully acknowledges their support.